P9-DMD-845

Willie's Wonderful Pet

by Mel Cebulash
Illustrated by George Ford

Hello Reader!

SCHOLASTIC INC.

New York   Toronto   London   Auckland   Syndey

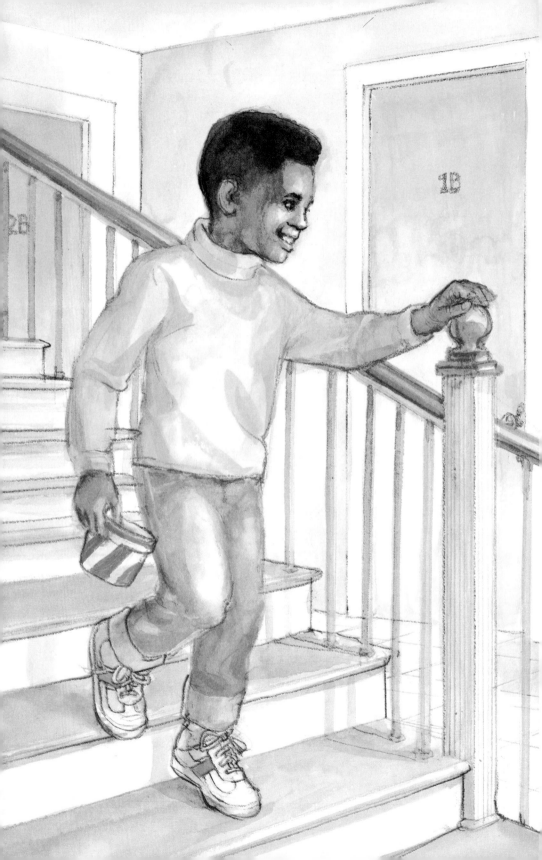

Willie and Wendy were
in the same class.
And they lived in the same building.
One day Willie said, "Tomorrow is
Pet Day."

Wendy said, "Why did you say you would bring a pet? You don't have a pet."

"But I'm going to get a pet," Willie said. "I'm going to the park to get a worm.
Do you want to come with me?"
"Yes," Wendy said. "No one will have a pet worm."

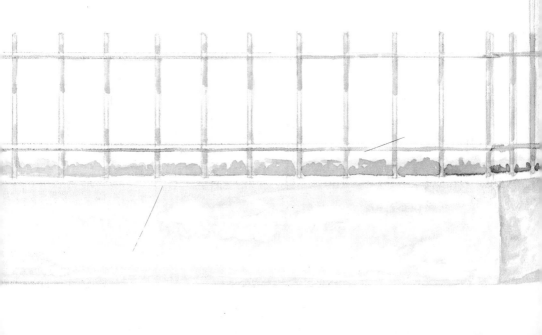

That afternoon they went

to the park.

Willie found a worm.

He found two worms.

But he put one back.

Wendy didn't want it.

The next day many
boys and girls had
their pets in class.

Al had his dog.

Cathy had her cat.

Henry had his rabbit.

George had his goldfish.

Rita had her bird.

And Mike had his hamster.

Willie had a paper cup
filled with dirt.

"What do you have, Willie?" Al asked.

"A worm," Willie said.

"What can he do?" asked Rita.

"I don't think he can do anything,"
Willie said.

"Then he's not a real pet," Mike said.

It was time for the pet show.

Miss Street said, "Willie, let us see your pet."

Willie showed his worm.

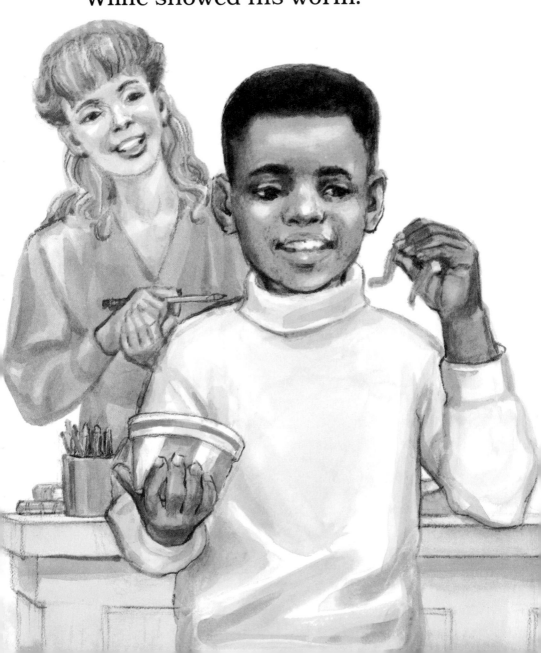

Miss Street asked, "What can he do?"

"Nothing," Willie said.

"I'm sure he can do something,"

Miss Street said. "You think about it."

Then Miss Street said, "Rita, what can your pet do?"

"My bird can sing," said Rita.

But Rita's bird wouldn't sing.
And the other pets wouldn't do
anything.
Then Willie said, "I know! My worm
can crawl!"

Willie put his worm on the floor.

Everybody watched.

The little worm crawled and crawled.

Then...

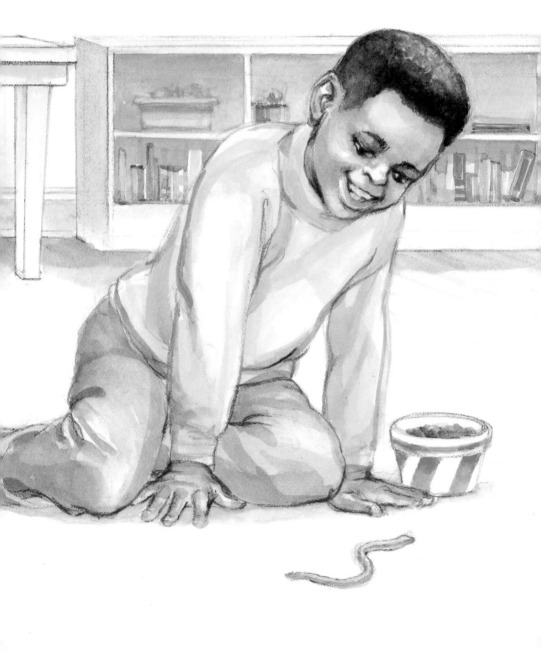

Al's dog barked.

And Cathy's cat jumped.

Henry's rabbit hopped.

And George's goldfish came to the top of the bowl.

Rita's bird sang.

And Mike's hamster ran around.

"Willie's pet can do more
than crawl," said Wendy.

"He can get things STARTED!"

A NOTE TO PARENTS

Reading Aloud with Your Child

Research shows that reading books aloud is the single most valuable support parents can provide in helping children learn to read.

- Be a ham! The more enthusiasm you display, the more your child will enjoy the book.
- Run your finger underneath the words as you read to signal that the print carries the story.
- Leave time for examining the illustrations more closely; encourage your child to find things in the pictures.
- Invite your youngster to join in whenever there's a repeated phrase in the text.
- Link up events in the book with similar events in your child's life.
- If your child asks a question, stop and answer it. The book can be a means to learning more about your child's thoughts.

Listening to Your Child Read Aloud

The support of your attention and praise is absolutely crucial to your child's continuing efforts to learn to read.

- If your child is learning to read and asks for a word, give it immediately so that the meaning of the story is not interrupted. DO NOT ask your child to sound out the word.
- On the other hand, if your child initiates the act of sounding out, don't intervene.
- If your child is reading along and makes what is called a miscue, listen for the sense of the miscue. If the word "road" is substituted for the word "street," for instance, no meaning is lost. Don't stop the reading for a correction.
- If the miscue makes no sense (for example, "horse" for "house"), ask your child to reread the sentence because you're not sure you understand what's just been read.
- Above all else, enjoy your child's growing command of print and make sure you give lots of praise. *You are your child's first teacher—and the most important one. Praise from you is critical for further risk-taking and learning.*

—Priscilla Lynch
Ph.D., New York University
Educational Consultant

To Ellen, Flo, and Marianne—
who undoubtedly would have taken the other worm
—M.C.

For Tom Feelings, to whom we all owe so much
—G.F.

Text copyright © 1972 by Mel Cebulash.
Illustrations copyright © 1993 by George Ford.
All rights reserved. Published by Scholastic Inc.
HELLO READER is a registered trademark of Scholastic Inc.
CARTWHEEL BOOKS is a trademark of Scholastic Inc.

No part of this publication may be reproduced in whole or in part, or stored
in a retrieval system, or transmitted in any form or by any means, electronic,
mechanical, photocopying, recording, or otherwise, without written
permission of the publisher. For information regarding permission, write
to Scholastic Inc., 730 Broadway, New York, NY 10003.

Library of Congress Cataloging-in-Publication Data

Cebulash, Mel.
  Willie's wonderful pet / by Mel Cebulash ; illustrated by George Ford.
    p.   cm. — (Hello reader)
  Summary: Willie's unusual pet helps make the class Pet Day a success.
  ISBN 0-590-45787-X
  [1. Pets—Fiction.] I. Ford, George Cephas, ill. II. Title. III. Series.
PZ7.C2997W1 1993
[E]—dc20   91-44270
                                       CIP
                                       AC

5 6 7 8 9 10   **09**   00 99 98 97 96 95 94

Printed in the U.S.A

First Scholastic printing, March 1993

THE END

*H*ello, Reader!

*Th*ese great stories are just for you!

Level 1
THE BUNNY HOP
"BUZZ," SAID THE BEE
ITCHY, ITCHY CHICKEN POX
MONKEY SEE, MONKEY DO
WILLIE'S WONDERFUL PET

Level 2
ALL TUTUS SHOULD BE PINK
THE FROG PRINCE
HARRY HATES SHOPPING!
KENNY AND THE LITTLE KICKERS
MORE SPAGHETTI, I SAY!
N—O SPELLS NO!
ROLLER SKATES!
THE SWORD IN THE STONE
TWO CRAZY PIGS
THE WRONG-WAY RABBIT

Level 3
THE BLIND MEN AND THE ELEPHANT
THAT FAT HAT
THE WITCH GOES TO SCHOOL

Level 1

*How to Choose a **Hello Reader!***		
Level 1:	Preschool–Grade 1	Ages 3–6
Level 2:	Kindergarten–Grade 2	Ages 5–7
Level 3:	Grades 1 & 2	Ages 6–8
Level 4:	Grades 2 & 3	Ages 7–9

Hello, Parent!

Hello Reader! books have been designed—

- for parents to read to children
- for children to read to parents
- for children to read themselves

—to make your child a better reader.

High-interest stories make reading fun! Stories have been tested for vocabulary and sentence length to help you make the right choice! A letter from an education specialist gives you valuable advice on how to read to your child and how to listen to your child read to you!

You are your child's first teacher…*the most important one!*
— Priscilla Lynch, Ph.D.

50295

9 780590 457873

ISBN 0-590-45787-X

Cartwheel
·B·O·O·K·S· ™

SCHOLASTIC INC.